# Sammy's New Friends

May you always love making new friends!

Linda K. Bridges 2018

Dedicated to Sammy & Seth, Carina, Simon, Noémie, Ellis, Romeo, Remy and Connor who just made new friends with Sammy Bunny and Red Fox and for whom this story was first told.

# Sammy's New Friends

written & illustrated by

Linda K. Bridges

Critter Creations

# Sammy Bunny's Family

Sammy lived with his family in the old, oak tree in the middle of the Big Woods.

He had lots of brothers and sisters:
Seth, Simon, Nina, Nomsie, and little Ellis.
Mama and Papa loved their bunnies
very much.

Can you count them?

On sunny days the Bunny children
played games together in the meadow.
Each one loved to hop and play
under the sun.

They had races, and each bunny tried very hard to be the fastest. Sammy hopped higher and ran faster than all the others.

More than racing or hopping,
Sammy loved to make new friends.
Everywhere he went, he wondered,
Who will be my friend today?

# Sammy's Hiding Place

One warm summer day, Sammy and his friends decided to play Hide-and-Seek in the woods near their meadow. Each bunny scattered to find the best hiding place.

Can you see where some of Sammy's friends are hiding?

Sammy discovered an old, hollow tree stump. Here it was quiet and dark. “This will be a good place to hide,” Sammy said. “No one will ever find me here!”

"No one can find me either!" said Snail.

After a long time, Sammy felt squirmy. He hopped quietly from his hiding tree to look around. He scratched his ear.

“Where is everybody?”
Sammy wondered out loud.

Sammy hopped a little farther.
A cracking noise made him stand very still.
Suddenly, Sammy heard a familiar voice.
"I see you!" shouted his brother, Seth.
Sammy jumped into the air! He tried to run,
but he was not fast enough.
Seth tagged him.

"Caught you, caught you!" Seth laughed.
The others giggled too.
"Ha-ha-ha! Now you are it!"
Sammy shrugged. He was caught,
even though he had the best hiding place!

"That's okay, Sammy! Everybody gets caught sometime!" Mouse squeaked.

Their game was over.
They joined Papa Bunny in the meadow.
On the way home, Sammy told Papa
about playing Hide-and-Seek.
It had been such a fun day!

## Sammy's Strange Meeting

One bright morning, Sammy rose earlier than usual. He and Mouse packed their lunch and took a walk in the Big Woods.

Sammy said to Mouse,
"I wonder who we will meet today?"
"Maybe Hildie Hedgehog," replied Mouse,
as they walked along the trail.
He liked Hildie!

Before long, Sammy and Mouse saw someone standing in the path ahead of them.

It was RED FOX.

He was big and strong, and his long tail flowed out behind him. “He is magnificent!” whispered Sammy.

Suddenly, Red Fox turned and stared right at Sammy and Mouse. He was smiling a little. Sammy wanted to be friends. Maybe Red Fox will play with us today, thought Sammy.
"Hello, Mr. Red Fox," said Sammy boldly.
"My name is Sammy Bunny.
Would you play with us?"

Red Fox looked hard at the little bunny.
Then he looked at Mouse.
He blinked and shook his head.
"I don't have time to play today."
With these words, he turned and ran
into the dark woods. Sammy and Mouse
stood looking at the spot where Red Fox
disappeared.

Sammy sat on a big rock. He sighed.
He thought about playing with Red Fox.
Mouse thought about Red Fox too.
"I wish I were big and strong like Red Fox!"
said Sammy Bunny.
"But I am just a little, brown bunny."

"Brown bunnies are VERY special,"
squeaked Mouse. "You can run and
hop faster than anyone, Sammy."

Sammy did not hear his friend's small voice.
He was too busy thinking. He jumped up.
"Come on! I have an idea.
Let's follow Red Fox."
Before Mouse and Snail could answer,
Sammy was running as fast as he could.
"Wait for me!" called Mouse.

"Go on! I will catch up with you!" called Snail, trailing behind them.

## Sammy's New Friends!

Sammy and Mouse followed Red Fox's trail until it disappeared. Then Sammy saw the old fallen tree stump in the clearing where he had hid.

Today, they were surprised to find a mother fox with her two kits playing there. Sammy and Mouse hid behind the rocks and watched. The little foxes were having so much fun. Sammy wanted to join them.

Finally, he could stand it no longer!
He hopped out and waved at them.
“Hello! My name is Sammy Bunny.
Will you play with me?”

Mother Fox and the kits stopped moving.
They looked at Sammy.

"Hello!" he said a little louder.
"May I play with you?"

"Hello!" squeaked Mouse.
"My name is Mouse."

Soon, Sammy, Mouse and their new friends were laughing and playing together. They tickled each other. They ran, hopped and jumped. Then the sunlight in the Big Woods began to fade. "Sammy, it is time to go home," said Mouse.

Just as they were leaving, a dark shadow crossed their path. It was Red Fox!

Sammy's new friends ran to Red Fox, yipping loudly. They were so happy to see their papa. He licked them with foxy kisses. Then he said, "Welcome, Sammy Bunny to our den. I see you and my sons had fun playing together." Red Fox swished his magnificent tail.

"Yes, Sir!" said Sammy. "We did have fun." Sammy felt happy inside. Red Fox was his friend too! "It's time for us to go home now," said Sammy. "Good-bye, little foxes. Good-bye, Mr. and Mrs. Fox."

As Sammy Bunny and Mouse scampered toward the old, oak tree in the middle of the Big Woods, Snail came slowly down the path. Sammy scooped him up. He wanted to get home fast so he could tell Mama and Papa Bunny all about his new friends!

The End

Many thanks to my husband, Al, who listened to untold variations of 'Sammy's New Friends' and was patient and helpful through the whole process.

Thanks to my dearest friend, Kristin, for encouraging me in so many ways to continue on, who loved the Bunny children's skinny arms and toothy smiles!

Thanks to my son, Jared, and daughter-in-law, Lori, who read, critiqued, formatted and gave valuable advice to make this story book the best book possible.

Thanks to my writing buddy, Cindy, for believing in me.



ISBN 978-0692360064



Genre: Fiction, Early Childhood illustrated storybook.

Illustrated on Strathmore Windpower Mixed Media vellum paper with watercolor wash, pen and ink.

## ABOUT THE AUTHOR:

Linda K. Bridges was born and raised in Bakersfield, California. She married her husband of 45 years, in 1969, and together they moved to Europe in 1978. They lived in Vienna, Austria for 15 years before returning to the United States. After their kids were grown they spent 5 years living in Thailand. Together they raised four children and now have nine grandchildren.

Linda describes herself as 'a bit of a late-bloomer' in the field of writing and illustrating children's storybooks, but nevertheless, believes deeply that it's never too late to start working on your dreams. Sammy's New Friends is her first book published under the trade name, Critter Creations.

Linda lives with her husband and their serendipitous critter, Sherlock (a miniature schnauzer), in Colorado Springs, Colorado.

You can follow Linda at www.lindakbridges.com to see what else she is working on.

81736418R00022

Made in the USA
Lexington, KY
20 February 2018